THE BRAVEST OF BEARS

For Linda, Marc, Luke and Holly

Text copyright ©1993 by John McClelland. Illustrations copyright ©1993 by Jooce Garrett.
This paperback edition first published in 2001 by Andersen Press Ltd. The rights of John McClelland and Jooce Garrett
to be identified as the author and illustrator of this work have been asserted by them
in accordance with the Copyright, Designs and Patents Act, 1988.
First published in Great Britain in 1993 by Andersen Press Ltd., 20 Vauxhall Bridge Road, London SW1V 2SA.
Published in Australia by Random House Australia Pty., 20 Alfred Street, Milsons Point, Sydney, NSW 2061.
All rights reserved. Colour separated in Switzerland by Photolitho AG, Zurich.
Printed and bound in China.

10 9 8 7 6 5 4 3 2 1

British Library Cataloguing in Publication Data available.

ISBN 0 86264 389 9

This book has been printed on acid-free paper

THE BRAVEST OF BEARS

Written by
JOHN McCLELLAND

Illustrated by
JOOCE GARRETT

Ⓐ
Andersen Press · London

THERE WAS once an old man who owned a toy shop. It wasn't very big and he didn't sell many toys. But he was happy.

The toys were happy too, for when the old man cleaned and tidied he talked to them softly to make them feel at home and when he sold them he made sure it was only to kind children.

One day, the old man became very ill and had to go to hospital. Soon afterwards a *For Sale* sign appeared on the front of the shop and all the toys were taken away by men in brown coats and never seen again.

All except one, that is. A tiny bear bravely climbed to the darkest, dustiest, highest and loneliest shelf in the shop and hid himself. There he sat, keeping very still so as not to be noticed, and waited for the old man to return.

The shop was sold to a crabbity-faced woman who filled it with mouldy pictures and worn out things.
Tiny Bear looked down . . .
He didn't like the look of the woman's crabbity face and he certainly couldn't understand why she had cluttered the shop with such rubbish.

He kept very still and wished she would go away.

She did eventually – for the shop was not a success.

A young man bought it and turned it into a boutique full of startling clothes. Startling people came to buy them. The young man played loud music and hopped, twitched and jumped all day long.

Tiny Bear peeked down . . .

The startling people and the loud music *and* the young man made him feel dizzy. He kept very still and hoped he wouldn't be sick.

Eventually the music stopped and the young man hopped, twitched and jumped away – for the shop was not a success.

Two jolly women moved in and opened a launderette
where lonely people came to wash their clothes.
Machines thundered day and night. The lonely people
coughed horribly and the two jolly women sang at the tops
of their voices.
Tiny Bear peeked down . . .
and sighed. He couldn't get any sleep and he wondered if
his friend, the old man, would ever come back.
The launderette was a great success and the two jolly
women made lots of money.

Then they began quarrelling and shouting at each other.
The shop was soon for sale again.

This time a quiet man with a bald head and a
cardigan started a Post Office.
Tiny Bear peeked down . . .
He thought the stamps were beautiful and the
bald man pleasantly quiet. Then a terrible thing
happened. Two robbers burst into the shop and
stole all the poor man's money.

Tiny Bear hid himself fearfully – for he was too
small to help – and after the robbers had gone the
quiet man went too.

No one bought the shop.

The building grew tired and fell into disrepair.
Mice ran everywhere, rats gnawed at the floor and the
windows were boarded.
It was dark inside.
Tiny Bear did not peek down . . .
He kept very still and tried not to breathe lest a dangerous
creature might find him.

Many months passed. Tiny Bear felt sad and very lonely.
Even though he was the bravest of bears, tears plopped
from his eyes and his little chest heaved with such sighs it
was certain his heart would break.

Until –

one summer's day when the door opened and a kind looking girl walked into the shop. She swept and cleaned, dusted and polished, painted and scrubbed till the old place looked like new. Then she carried in boxes and parcels, packages and bags, cases and tea chests. She began to unpack them.

Tiny Bear looked down . . .
and smiled.
There were toys littering the floor,
there were toys filling the shelves,
there were toys crowding into the
windows.
They were happy toys for, as the
girl worked, she spoke to them
softly to make them feel at home.

That night, when she had left, Tiny Bear climbed down to one of the shelves and snuggled in between a doll and a baby elephant. The doll shifted away (for Tiny Bear *was* rather dirty) but the elephant wrapped him up in his trunk and gave him a friendly squeeze.

Next morning the girl brought her grandfather to attend the GRAND OPENING. She wheeled him in in a chair all swaddled in blankets and rugs.

Tiny Bear peeked down . . . and clapped his paws excitedly. It was the old man come home and the first thing *he* saw was *his* Tiny Bear – dirty, dusty and grinning.

The old man reached down to his friend, clutched him gently to his chest, and spoke to him softly.
The two were never parted again.

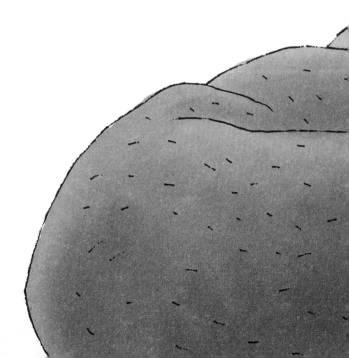